I Love You, Blue Kangaroo!

Emma Chichester Clark

HarperCollins *Children's Books*

for
Lily Brown
and her little brother
Jack

Have you read these picture books by Emma Chichester Clark?

Where Are You, Blue Kangaroo?

It Was You, Blue Kangaroo!

What Shall We Do, Blue Kangaroo?

I'll Show You, Blue Kangaroo!

Merry Christmas, Blue Kangaroo!

Happy Birthday, Blue Kangaroo!

Follow My Leader!

No More Kissing!

First published as a Hardback in Great Britain by Anderson Press Ltd in 1998
First published as a paperback by Picture Lions in 2000
The edition published by HarperCollins Children's Books in 2009

1 3 5 7 9 10 8 6 4 2

ISBN-13: 978-0-00-664684-6

Picture Lions is an imprint of HarperCollins Children's Books, which is a division of HarperCollins Publishers Ltd.

Text and illustrations copyright © Emma Chichester Clark 1998

Visit our website at: www.harpercollins.co.uk
Printed and bound in China

Blue Kangaroo belonged to Lily.
He was her very own kangaroo.
Every night, Lily said,
"I love you, Blue Kangaroo!"
And Blue Kangaroo fell fast asleep in Lily's arms.

Then one day, Lily's Aunt Jemima came to tea.
She gave Lily a wild brown bear.

He was huggable and furry with wild, brown eyes.

That night, Lily took the wild brown bear
up to bed with her. She said,
"I love Wild Brown Bear...

...and I love you, Blue Kangaroo!"

Blue Kangaroo
didn't sleep quite
so well after that.

The next Saturday, Lily's mother's friend, Florence, came to tea. She gave Lily a yellow cotton rabbit.

He was floppy and fleecy with velvety ears.

That night, as Lily got ready for bed, she said,
"I love Yellow Cotton Rabbit...

...I love Wild Brown Bear,
and I love you, Blue Kangaroo!"

Blue Kangaroo
hardly slept at all
after that.

Then Roly Poly Uncle George came to stay.
He gave Lily two furry puppies.

They were cuddly and fluffy with shiny black noses.

That night, as Lily put her pyjamas on, she said,
"I love the Furry Puppies...

...I love Yellow Cotton Rabbit,
I love Wild Brown Bear,
and I love you, Blue Kangaroo!"

After that,
Blue Kangaroo
hardly slept a wink.

On Lily's birthday, Mrs Appleby gave Lily
a wiggly green crocodile, and her Great Uncle Arthur

gave her a long-eared owl.
Lily's cousin, Amelia, gave her a little, tiny teddy.

That night, as Lily brushed her teeth, she said,
"I love Tiny Teddy, I love Long-Eared Owl,
I love Wiggly Green Crocodile...

...I love the Furry Puppies,
I love Yellow Cotton Rabbit,
I love Wild Brown Bear,
and I love you, Blue Kangaroo!"

Blue Kangaroo lay
on the edge of the bed
and stared at the ceiling.

In the middle of the night, Lily rolled over.
Then Tiny Teddy rolled over.
Then Long-Eared Owl rolled over.
Then Wiggly Green Crocodile rolled over.

Then the Furry Puppies rolled over.
Then Yellow Cotton Rabbit rolled over.
Then Wild Brown Bear rolled over...

...and Blue Kangaroo rolled out of bed, onto the floor.
He looked up at Lily and the sleeping creatures.

"There's just no room for me anymore," he said sadly,
and he hopped across the carpet and out of the door.

He hopped along the passage
to the baby's room,
and he hopped up
into the baby's warm cot.

"Goo goo, boo gangaloo!"
gurgled the baby
as he squeezed Blue Kangaroo
tightly in his little pink fists.

The next day, Lily looked everywhere
for Blue Kangaroo.
"Goo goo, boo gangaloo!" cooed the baby.

"Mine!" cried the baby.
"No!" shouted Lily.

"Lily!" said her mother. "You've got so many animals.
Surely you can let the baby have just one?"
"Not Blue Kangaroo!" cried Lily.

Lily ran to her room and when she came back,
her arms were full.
"He can have all of these," she said,
"but nobody can have Blue Kangaroo!"

That night, the baby went to bed with
the wild brown bear, the yellow cotton rabbit,
the furry puppies, the wiggly green crocodile,
the long-eared owl and the little, tiny teddy.

Lily went to bed with Blue Kangaroo.
Blue Kangaroo snuggled up to Lily. She stroked his
blue ears, then she kissed the tip of his soft blue nose.
"I love you Blue Kangaroo!" she said...

...and Blue Kangaroo
fell fast asleep
in her arms.